D1559278

Wherever the Wind Blows Me...

Laurie Elizabeth Murphy

Wherever the Wind Blows Me...

A Chronicle of Friendship

SPARROW HEART PUBLISHING

Published by Sparrow Heart Publishing

ISBN-13: 978-0-615-60554-8

James Ferraro
Cover Designer, Consigliere
Architect of Dreams, Amateur Hoarder

Mary Gerth
Technical Support and Marketing

This book is available as an e-book and in paperback.
For paperback orders, please call (772) 283-8558, or write to:

SPARROW HEART PUBLISHING
421 South East Martin Avenue
Stuart, Florida 34996

First Edition, March 4, 2012

DEDICATION

This book is dedicated to Bonnie Banker Singer, and our friendship of over 46 years. She's taught me everything I know about humility, strength, courage, stamina and perseverance.

We met at the Mount Sinai Hospital School of Nursing in New York City, and not only survived the next three years of impossible classes and work schedules, but found an affordable apartment in Manhattan following graduation. By then, the world was mine to own. By then, fate stepped in and dealt her an unfair hand. Time has taken its toll. I hope she can still remember that it was she who kept our apartment orderly and clean, made certain that the rent was paid on time, and that our fridge was stocked with food. She has an infectious laugh, a compassionate heart, and rhythm. That girl could really dance!

As so often happens with long-distance friendships, even the most well-intentioned plans of remaining in touch become riddled with years of absences. Mostly, these are my offenses, not hers. She not only continues to forgive my broken promises, but thanks me each time I call. I know I don't deserve her friendship, but I am forever grateful. Her life's path has been incredibly difficult, but she has always handled it with dignity and grace.

God bless you, Pookie. You are a true role model, a great friend, and my hero.

ACKNOWLEDGMENT

As always, I am thankful for Divine Intervention, placing us where we need to be, when we need to be there.

INTRODUCTION

This is the story of friendship, carved out by the universe—destined. It is the coming together of two unlikely souls, colliding in a celestial moment and setting in motion the rest of their lifes' journey.

It is only true if you believe it is, and sad, only if you cannot see past tomorrow.

Wherever the Wind Blows Me...

CHAPTER ONE

I am not pleased. It appears that someone has purchased the little house that sits next door to where I live. The house that I wanted to buy. I haven't seen them yet, but there is action going on. A car in the driveway, a light over the front door. Mowed grass. It has been empty for so long, I just assumed it would always be there, waiting for me.

In truth, I couldn't have bought it. I know that. Everyone I ever told of my intentions knew that. Still, it could have happened. People win stuff. I could have won something, money or something. Then I could have made a serious offer. Then I could maybe, someday, buy that house.

I wonder who they are. Most likely pretentious. This is a pretentious neighborhood. Maybe young, a nosey woman

1

who gossips too much. A man who lifts weights and drinks before five. The house is small. Maybe an older couple, retired. A couple who hates noise, and children. And dogs.

From the beginning, there was something about the little house. It just sits there, unassuming. Expecting nothing. Proud, but neglected. It calls to me when I walk in the cul-de-sac. Notice me, it yearns. I do, I say. I think you're beautiful. It blushes with embarrassment, and stands a little taller.

And now this. Strangers, coming to defile my house. Coming with their negativity and tensions, their emotional baggage and material worthlessness. I will put a curse on the house, I think. I know absolutely nothing about curses, but still, I close my eyes and wish really hard that they will go away. But when I open my eyes, their car is still there.

It doesn't matter who they are, I think. They can be nice, or mean, friendly or hostile. They can be young or old, healthy or sickly. Regardless of their life circumstances, they can keep their stories to themselves. I am not interested in hearing about places they've traveled or hobbies they've mastered. I don't much care about people they have met along the way. I don't like them.

CHAPTER TWO

Their lights have been on for the past two weeks, but I can't see much of anything through the windows. When I take the garbage cans out to the street, I face forward but my eyes dart to the right, struggling to catch a glimpse of the people I hate. There is noise. A lot of noise. Hammering, mostly. Late at night, which is against the ordinances of our snooty community, but they don't know enough to quiet down, or they don't care. I don't care either. Neither does anyone else in the circle. Maybe they're renters, fixing up the place for a year's stay before they move on. A year wouldn't be so bad. Less would be better.

CHAPTER THREE

I have never really committed to exercise, but since they've been here, I walk every evening, so as not to miss anything. Tonight I see a man dressed in work clothes. He looks at me, as if he wants to say something. He looks like a handyman. All sweaty and dirty. What would he have to say to me? More to the point, what would I have to say to him? I keep on walking, though truth be told, I should stop to ask about the renters. He probably knows plenty. Looks like he works until he gets tired, then he sleeps at the house. Must be some major renovations going on inside. Must be somebody rich who can afford to employ the handyman full time.

The next night I walk the circle again. I see the handyman. He waves, and I stop to talk. Do you know the owners? I ask. Yes, he says. Are they nice? I ask. Pretty nice, he says. Well, I'm not going to like them, I say. They're moving into my house. That's too bad, he says. They would have liked you.

Just like that, brazen and bold. Making assumptions about who might like whom. He should stick to putting in windows and door sills. He should take out the rot underneath the roof eves and not bother about my business.

The next night the handyman stands in the circle, staring at the little house. *My house.* He says hello, and waits for me to stop to chat. I appease him. What are they like, the couple moving in? I ask. He says the man's name is Rod, and he is a musician, and the lady's name is Julie, or something like that. The boy's name is Hawk, like the bird, which I find to be extremely suspicious. Why would a boy be named after a bird? He holds out his hand in greeting. I shake it. We exchange names. Rod, he says. My name is Rod.

Deception! I think. He deceived me by allowing me to think he was a handyman, when he turns out to be the new owner. He says his wife and child will follow along in a couple months, once the house is ready. I nod my head, as if I care, but I don't. I don't need another friend, especially not one who lies by omission. He should have told me straight away his relation to the house. He should have known I would mistake him for a worker. He should have introduced himself on day one. He should have stayed where he came from.

CHAPTER FOUR

The weather has turned cold. Florida cold. I haven't walked lately, so I suppose I have missed the arrival of Julie and The Bird. I stay to myself, mind my own business, go to work, come home, go to bed, and start all over again. I spend time with my husband and children. I spend time with my grandchildren. There's no more room for anyone else. So, that's that.

It's dark when I get home from work. Not late, really, but dark. Winter. But this one night, my little corner of the circle is aglow in lights. Christmas lights! I think. The little house has Christmas lights! But no! Instead of Christmas lights, they have hung a peace sign that nearly

11

covers the entire front wall of the little house, shining bright white, house dressing for the weary, reminders for lost souls, symbols of what we all could be, if only we all tried just a little harder.

My car idles in the street, facing the sign. I sit there watching time standing still, then flying backwards, reminding me of everything I had ever believed in: The West Village, my hippie dreams of crafting silver jewelry, writing poetry, and living in a loft. But that was when I was still young enough to be naïve and hopeful, nostalgic for another time and place.

And that is how Julie and I meet. The man, Rod, stands at his front door waving, cleaned up, majestic under the lights of his peace sign. He looks different. Better. Cleaner. His entire demeanor seems oddly transformed, confident, understanding, patient. Perhaps I have misjudged him. Or perhaps not. His cleanliness should not be my barometer to his character.

His wife walks over to my car, without hesitation, unwavering, on a path not yet revealed. She looks angelic, pure, sweet. Quiet confidence and grace follow her, daring to not fall behind, obedient in their loyalty. In that one instant I believe her to be revered, the keeper of the highest secrets.

I feel drawn to her. Before my thoughts can be censored, before my mind has enough sense to curb my words, this is what comes to me. This is what I hear myself saying inside my head. Thank God, you're finally here.

CHAPTER FIVE

I am annoyed that Julie has such a spell on me, a witch-like spell that tries to make me like her, but I will not give in. I will not be controlled by witchcraft. She can cast her spells on other people, weaker people, people who will fall for it. Not me. She will never control me.

She just keeps talking. I don't know what she is saying. I am fighting the spell, forcing myself to disengage. Her mouth keeps moving, words falling out. I say nothing until she finally stops. Silence hangs in the air. I reach for something civil, something superficial, friendly, pleasant,

15

but distant. But instead what I say only proves that she is forcing her will on me. This is what I say. Do you know anything about spoon bending?

I try to suck the words back in, but it's too late. Maybe it's the night air or the glow of lights. Maybe it is some past yearning of a Hippie lifestyle, but whatever it is, I actually ask this question to a perfect stranger. A question left over from my bucket list of 1999.

I expect her to be shocked, horrified. I am. I expect her to walk away, shut her blinds, lock her doors, and tell her child never to come near my property. Instead, quiet, she ponders my question, and then says no, she had never been successful at spoon-bending, but she thinks her husband might be, and perhaps one night, we could all give it a try.

Truly, that is what she says to me. Then she turns and walks back to her house. Just like that. Like our conversation is over. Like things are normal. They are anything but normal! Where the hell is she going with my words? To tell her husband about the lunatic who lives next door? How about her, coming out at night with no coat? Coming over to a stranger's car? Forcing me to say something I don't want to say? What about that?

I watch her walk into the house. I want to wish her permanently gone. I want to envision a moving van parked in her driveway loading up her belongings, taking her to some faraway place that I have never heard of, or at least can't locate on the map. Maybe Oregon, or Montana. I want to turn back time, make the house empty once more, and darken the street. That's what I tell myself. But the truth is I want to follow her. Just leave my car in the middle of the street and follow her. Then I want to beg her to be my friend.

I race into the house to tell my husband about her. I make a conscious effort to leave out the part about the spoon-bending. That's not his thing. She seems nice, I say. Huh, he says. I wouldn't get too friendly with the neighbors.

CHAPTER SIX

He isn't wrong. I know the rules. I made them. No friendships with anybody in close proximity, people who latch on like leeches, who will never go away, who have no respect for privacy. I don't want that, someone knowing my business, someone talking about me, judging me, striking up conversation like we have something in common, which we don't.

But she did seem nice. Nice in a way that someone is nice when they are trying to put a spell on me. And the spell seems to be working. I can't stop thinking about her. I try to ignore my overwhelming desire to see her. I drive past her house more slowly, still admiring the peace sign, going out for milk or bread, making runs to the bank, or dropping off dry cleaning. I go out as often as I can, pretending that I don't want to see her. But I do.

Now I am the one skulking about, driving the streets all hours of the day and night stealing a glance or two. I rush home from work, and park my car in the street with my headlights pointed into their living room window. Still they don't appear. What is their problem? I think. Are they hiding from me?

I keep an eye out for Julie and Rod in the circle. I wish I had a dog to walk. I want to see Julie in the daylight. I want to see what the sparkle was all about. The glitter. The fairy dust. These people are really beginning to get on my nerves. Why don't they just come out of their house? But when Florida turns cold, no one comes out of their house, even if the cold is no less than sixty degrees.

Occasionally she is there in the morning, standing by the curb, at the street, by her garbage cans, at the mailbox.

Sometimes she is there early, when I pick up my newspaper, and I act like I don't see her. She acts like she can't see me either. In fairness, I should tell you that she actually can't see me because I am standing behind a large bush. Because I am in my nightgown. I have spent the past ten years retrieving the paper in my nightgown. I'm not about to dress up for her. She can't make me change things for her.

But today I don't notice her. I don't take cover behind the bush. I bend down, in my nightgown, pick up the paper, and there she is. Just like that. Not less than five feet in front of me, wearing a nightgown, just like me! Is this her idea of a joke? Is she mocking me? How rude! I should turn around and walk away. I should call the newspaper and stop delivery immediately. She has no social graces. No social etiquette. You just don't sneak up on someone like this. Hi, she says. Hi, Julie, I say.

This morning ritual goes on for the better part of a week. If I get the paper at eight, she's there. If I wait until nine, she's there. If I don't pick it up until well after ten, there again. Four mornings in a row, we exchange greetings. Four mornings in a row she wears her nightgown. I know she and her deceptive husband are laughing at me. Behind my back. Laughing over my nightgown. I am completely offended. Then, on the fifth morning she announces that her name is Jill, not Julie. But you can call me Julie if you want to, she says.

I am mortified. And angry. Her husband did not say her name was Jill. At least, I don't think he did. Unless he mumbles. That could be a possibility. He looks like a man who might mumble. Or it is certainly possible that he is playing some sort of trick, a cruel joke, to make her not like me. A family of tricksters, that's what they are. Maybe he is getting back at me for thinking he is a handyman. But in order to know that I actually believed him to be a worker, rather than an owner, he would have had to read my mind. Is it possible that he is not only a spoon-bender but also a mind reader? That must be it, I think. A family of mind readers, vagabonds, spoon benders, and who knows what else? Still, I can't avoid them entirely. I am not about to place myself in a position that would be interpreted by them to be oppositional, not if my fate rests in their hands, their spells, their wizardry.

As a protective measure, I decide I will call her Jill. After all, it is her name. Just as it should be.

CHAPTER SEVEN

Strangely, I feel some inner longing trying to break through. Something familiar from another time. Something I can't put my finger on. It's disconcerting. Jill has taken up lodging in my head, an uninvited resident, snarling my brains. A resident with one name I have to erase, and another that I have to remember.

I want to mind the rules. Neighbors are neighbors, not friends. Otherwise, the next thing you know, they make comments about your comings and goings. No sooner did I have that thought, than that is exactly what happened! On the ninth week, Rod is outside playing with his son. He waves. Then he comments about how I take the garbage cans to the street late at night. The gravel driveway amplifies the sound, he says. So what? I think. There's no garbage can curfew. There's no law about the time of night you can take out your garbage. I don't comment about his hammering all night long. Mind your business, I think.

If they know about my garbage can ritual, what else do they know? What about my schedule? My predictable schedule. Should they assume that I have no plans on a Saturday night if my car remains in the driveway? Will they talk behind my back on Sunday morning if I don't go to Church? Should I start being more faithful about going to Church just so that they don't talk? No, I think. That's how Jill will control me. It's already starting. But I should go to Church, I want to go to Church, but now I don't know my real intentions. Am I going because I want to give them nothing to talk about, or because I really want to go? Does it matter? Does it count, with God, I mean, if I go to satisfy my own paranoia?

I feel conflicted. And crazy. They really are making me crazy. I don't need this. I am going to do the exact opposite of what I think they think I should do, to defy their super-powers. This has gone too far. They are sucking the air out of my space.

Still, I wonder if there is any chance that she could be my friend. If she would like me. I feel so torn, twisted by my own sanctions. It is tempting to let her into my life. I feel embarrassed that I am so desperate to have a friend. I wish they never moved here. I was doing fine without them. My head hurts. My heart hurts.

CHAPTER EIGHT

I'm back on track. I did a lot of thinking last night and pushed Jill right out of my mind. Got rid of the whole flim-flam family. My life is predictable, just the way I like it. Just the way it should be. I get up, go to work, come home, clean the house, cook dinner, go to bed, and get up the next day. That's it. It's called adulthood. It's apparently what the neighbors haven't learned, from what I can tell. They really just don't have the first clue.

Don't get me wrong. I used to daydream. When I was about seven or thirteen. I know about giggling until my stomach hurts, the high of a first love, and obsessing about endless possibilities of saving the world, feeding the hungry, being discovered, writing the great American novel.

I believe in the magic of childhood. I believe in Santa Claus. I believe in the goodness of mankind. But I don't have time for all that right now. I have responsibilities. I have a job. I have children and grandchildren. I have important places to be, commitments, people who demand my time.

They play. That's what I think. There's way too much fun going on next door. They need to grow up. They need to turn down the volume on the laughter pouring out of their house. There are serious things going on in the world. Nothing is that funny. Not anymore. Not when there are bills to be paid, and obligations that multiply by the minute. They should feel what I feel. Career demands that strangle me like a tight collar squeezing my neck, choking the life out of me. They need to join the ranks of those of us who have lost our way, taken the wrong path, and continue accumulating regrets. Some of us are up to our eyeballs in regrets. They need to get real.

And they need to ratchet down the music pouring out of their living room. No one wants to hear it. Don't they care that it's spilling onto the street, floating through the air, bouncing off on my windowsill, bothering the neighbors? Taunting me? Something is definitely wrong with them.

And the next time I talk to them, I'm going to mention that no one appreciates people flaunting too much free time. What's their game? As far as I can tell, Jill and Rod don't go to work. Bird Boy doesn't go to school. They seem to completely avoid the social rules of nature. Adults go to work, children attend school. Instead, they do a lot of entertaining. Cars, coming in and out of the street, parking all cockeyed. People carrying wine. Staying late. Sometimes all night. Just what are they up to?

I am tied to my life. It is imprinted in indelible ink on acid free paper. Truly. My entire life is etched in an appointment book that dictates every hour of my day. That book owns me.

They must think they're so great. They apparently feel no shame in staying home, dabbling in the arts, spending days creating ideas, sharing friendships with wine and food, staying up late and sleeping in. Who does that? Who wants to?

But then, I think, I do. I want to do what they do. I want permission to be footloose. I want the luxury of sitting around the house listening to music, painting, taking photographs. I want to refinish furniture, or spend all afternoon discovering various types of teas and coffees. I want to be them.

I am obsessed with finding out what makes them tick. Suddenly, I am the neighbor peeking through my blinds, watching them. I am the one making judgments, inventing scenarios, monitoring their comings and goings. I am the spy, I am the invader of privacy. I am the eraser of boundaries. I can't help it. I feel lonely for her.

CHAPTER NINE

They are changing my house. Her house. Painting it. Planting flowers of every color and variety. Pressure cleaning the roof. Moving the mailbox, adding a lamp post. It looks great. Really great. Now, when I walk in the circle, the house doesn't need my approval. It looks confident. It feels proud. I am happy that it's happy.

They are busy every day, the people next door. They paint, they clean, they talk on their cell phones out in the yard. And yet, they are happy. Even with their shirt sleeves rolled up, and their clothes messed with the grime of chores, they seem happy. When they see me, they drop their hoses, or shovels, stop what they're doing, and wave. They always wave. Hi Jill, I call across the yards. She smiles. She is still sprinkled in fairly dust. Glitter still floats around her. I am not quite as worried about being under her spell, although I haven't completely dismissed the idea. Jill, the good witch. It's a possibility.

The boy, Hawk, rings my bell every night. Without exception. Mostly for nothing in particular. He is sweet, smart, and creative. He crafts rocket-ships from pen parts and fighter planes from Lego's. He comes to stuff his pockets with bubble gum from my machine. In return, he brings me treasures from his toy chest. You can keep them, he says. Tonight, he brings me a marble given to him by his grandfather. I know I shouldn't take it. But I do.

Hawk wears the innocent face of the future, before the future became grim with statistics of corruption and violence. He carries hope in his bucket, and love in his heart. He has a mop of blonde, wavy hair and wears pukka beads around his neck. A four-foot high barefoot surfer dude. His face is his mother's. His inventions his fathers. His courage and fearlessness, gifts from both parents. He eagerly shares his imagination with me, unaware that we are nearly six decades apart. He seems older than his years, wiser than a six year old. Perhaps even wiser than me.

He invites me to dinner. His own invitation, not his parents. I decline. His face is laden with hurt feelings. Please, he begs. My mom and dad don't care. I want to take him in my arms and hug him, but I don't. He looks like he wishes I did.

I want to change my clothes, fix my hair, and follow this child home. I want to be seated at his table as an invited guest. I wanted to be part of his family for one hour, one night, or maybe forever. Maybe his mother isn't a witch. He doesn't seem like the child of a woman who casts spells. He seems innocent, and pure. I watch him walk away without me and try to wish him back.

CHAPTER TEN

This whole Jill-experience has me feeling out of sorts. Like someone else. Someone cynical and suspicious and angry. When did I become so possessive of my time? So shut down that I have sealed all entrances into my life, making it impossible for anyone to penetrate. I don't want to examine old wounds, but they are reopening despite me. Wounds caused by friends. Wounds caused by me.

So many of my friends have drifted away, leaving with the same promise to stay in touch, believing that no amount of geographical distance can destroy the bond, but it does. Distance matters, no matter what. Distance robs people of the back story of daily life. Explanation is wearisome. Phone calls become a chore. There is a pattern to loss. Christmas cards become less newsy, more generic. Then the calls and cards are noticeably absent, and it is a bittersweet relief, one less thing to worry about, to make time for. I don't hear much news from my old friends anymore. I secretly blame them, but in truth, I am the one who doesn't make the effort, who has turned away.

I hate that about me.

And now, I feel the pattern repeating. Another person I am about to invest in. Another disappointment brewing just around the corner. But there is no turning back. Every day I see her watching me from the window. Watching, as I retrieve my newspaper. If I keep my distance now, I think, it might not be too late. I might have a chance to back out. Now I don't want to run into her anymore. I make a silent pledge to close that window. The risk is too great.

I feel angry at the paper boy. He should make more effort to get the paper to my door. That's his job. How difficult is it to throw a little farther? To use a little muscle. Why should it be my effort? In the heat. In the rain. Maybe his holiday tip was too little. Maybe I didn't give him one at all. I make a mental note to remember him next year. That done, I feel free to continue my tirade. Lazy, I think. The paper boy is careless and lazy. I should complain. I should make a phone call to his supervisor. I should report his ineptness. I could even have him fired. That one phone call could reroute his entire life. But I don't want to do that. I simply want my paper delivered to the door. It's not his fault that I want to hunker down inside my house and become invisible.

 ## CHAPTER ELEVEN

Today is the day that will change everything. I could not have anticipated the direction my life was about to take. But destiny will not be stopped.

Jill is standing at the curb. Right next to my paper. Hi, she says. Hi, I say. She looks at me with her sweet, angelic face, the very same one she gave to her son on the day of his birth.

There is no conversation other than what I am about to tell you. No preamble to the content. No preparation for what is coming. For no reason other than fate she says, I write movies. Oh, I say. I write books. She says, I have a book I need to write, but I don't know how. I can help you, I say.

Just like that. Instantly we are transformed from strangers to friends. Instinctively I trust her. We are propelled to a deeper level. I understand who she is. I forgive her anything that will ever need forgiving, and I expect that she will do the same for me.

You might say a friendship like this takes years, and even then... But this friendship has waited lifetimes to rekindle.

I have a message that needs to be told, she says. I have carried it in my head for three years. What is the message, I ask? That it is still possible to find happiness, to help others, to change what needs to be changed, and to get back in touch with what really matters. This is the message I need to be written, she says. Oh, I say. Yes, she says. After a long silence she asks, will you do it? Yes, I say.

The name of the book is Satori, she says. Oh, I say. I have never heard of Satori. I do not even know if this is a real word or one that she has invented. I do not know how to spell it, or what it means. I can't remember how to pronounce it only a few moments after she has told it to me. But I believe her. I believe it must be written.

42

When can we begin, she asks? Today, I say. Right now. She is thrilled, and so am I. Without the slightest hesitation we hug each other, to wipe away the distance and cement us.

We make a plan, or at least, I make a plan. I am a planner. I never used to be, but in my adult life, I have learned to plan. It is decided that during the day, she will tell me about her ideas, chapter by chapter. Then I will take the ideas and turn them into a manuscript. It is also decided that we will meet in the circle each morning to exchange ideas and manuscripts, one day following the next, until the project is complete.

I like the orderliness of the plan. We each know what must be done. We each know what is expected. This will be simple, I say. It won't take long. How long, she asks? No more than two months, I say. Three at the most.

CHAPTER TWELVE

I did not take into consideration what should have been somewhat apparent, in hindsight. Jill possesses many great qualities, but punctuality is not one of them. She can't help it. Time has no real meaning to her. Urgency escapes her. Deadlines float in some gray area, always pushed into the background of the next idea, the next interruption, the next dinner party.

My thinking is black and white. I make a decision and stick to it. My word is my bond. I mean what I say. Every time. I depend on deadlines to push me toward a goal. How else will I get things done? The plan we had mapped out lasts for approximately two days. Then, her attention turns elsewhere. While I write, she plans trips, she entertains, she is on the phone. Don't worry, she says. I am thinking about the book. I am formulating the chapters.

I am as frustrated by her lack of follow through as I am by my impatience. After all, I think, it is her book. It is her three-year burden. I have only just come on the scene to remove this book from her head. To save her. But I am beginning to wonder if she wants to be saved.

One day I corner Rod. I tell him of my frustrations. I plead with him to put her back on track. Why can't she uphold her end of the bargain? I ask. He stares at me for what seems a long time. He formulates his words carefully. His tone is serious, protective. He says, Jill is a wonderful woman. That's all. It is a warning that I am teetering on the invisible line between my criticism and his stance. He will not divide his loyalties. He will not allow any commentary that hits below the belt. I didn't mean anything by it, I say. Good, he says.

In the following days, there are no further trading of manuscripts. There are no corrections made by her, nor ideas for the next section of material. I am moving away from annoyance and heading toward anger. This is not my book, I think. I can't come up with ideas without her. I've never even heard of Satori before. But I know enough about it to know that the concept is peaceful. Her careless attitude is making me feel anything but peaceful.

I spend days wondering how to approach the subject with Jill. I do not want to hurt her feelings. Moreover, I do not want to anger her, tempt her wizardry, if in fact, she possesses any super-human qualities. And that is still a distinct possibility. There will have to be adjustments. My expectation of time frustrates her. Her lack of follow through frustrates me. She continues to smile, and remain calm. Her calmness sets me on a course of neurosis. I talk to myself. Out loud. I try to reason with Jill. Then I try yelling. Then I feel badly for yelling, so I apologize. Jill does not respond. She can't. She's not with me.

I settle on making excuses for her. She's busy. She's sick. Neither is true. I hint at my frustration, but she doesn't care. She doesn't even excuse herself. She feels no remorse that I am becoming disenchanted with this whole set up.

When I spend my time writing something I expect to have something to show for it. I have nothing. She hasn't come up with the material for weeks. I am beginning to wonder if she even knows what messages she hopes to convey. This book will never be finished.

There are long spans of time without progress. Spans that are filled with me muttering under my breath, thinking unpleasant thoughts, and forcing myself to find balance. But those long pauses in our work are not entirely bad. I think of those times now, and I am thankful for them. They gave us time to laugh, and talk. They gave us time to really get to know each other, to support each other's dreams, to gather possibilities.

Over the next several months, I began to let go, to allow myself to loosen up, to smile more, to realize that rushing time is pointless. Time will not be controlled. Time is a precious gift, as important to the human spirit as any achieved goal. Without knowing it, I was becoming de-conditioned from my harried life, transformed. I smile more. I sleep better. I feel well. I am nicer.

I listen to the rain as it hits the roof, watch the birds fly ahead of the storm, smell the freshness of wet grass, appreciate the darkness of the night, and the magic of flickering stars. I have missed so much, rushing. I am sorry I haven't noticed how tall you've become, I say to the trees in my yard. I've just been busy. That's all right, they say back to me. You're here now.

But there are still nights when I stare at blank pages and seethe with anger. I think of all the things I have neglected in order to allocate my time to this project. I wonder if Jill has thought about that. If she the capacity to see what I am going through from my eyes. Unspoken words. Unwritten messages. I vacillate from my world to Jill's, and back again. My world feels more productive. Hers feels better. In her world I am able to take a deep breath for the first time in a long time. In her world I realize that I have been holding my breath for most of my life.

Jill witnesses my growth. She sees me younger, more courageous, more viable. She sees the old me, before I hated to travel, before I grew into a junk food junkie, before

I was too lazy to exercise. She has magically turned back time. I am me again. I am not lost. She has found me. I am giddy with the realization that I haven't evaporated, but that my new form is lighter, unburdened. I am suddenly no longer obsessed with the book. It's incomplete state. I am more concerned with my completion. I have learned to pause in between sentences, and enjoy the space between destinations.

 **CHAPTER THIRTEEN**

So far, our encounters have taken place outside, in the circle. Today I am invited to come over to the house for a cup of tea. I am still wearing my pajamas, but I cannot miss the chance. I do not have time to dress. I am afraid she will change her mind. Walking over, I imagine overstuffed chairs with flowered prints, lace curtains tied back with ribbon, mahogany furniture covered with crocheted doilies. I imagine myself perched on a nearby foot stool next to the silver tea set, with porcelain cups and scones on good china dishes. We will talk and eat, while all the time I will be gathering information, searching for clues, looking for signs of crystal balls, or potions.

The husband, Rod, does not seem to notice my attire. He stands brewing fresh tea at the kitchen counter, mixing leaves of orange spice and jasmine pearls, serving it gracefully. Three of us sit at a high top table, sipping tea with honey, discussing the essence of life, and the hazards, or pleasures, depending who is making the case, of drinking soda. We take opposing sides on the talents of Elvis Presley, consider the importance of home-schooling, and agree upon the urgent need for universal peace.

I feel quite Zen, although I don't actually know what that means. But I do find an inner peace, among the browns and greens that define the walls and floors. I feel soothed by the outdoorsy colors. I feel real, stripped of anything fake, and plastic. There are no floral prints and doilies. But there is something. Forms configure on the wall, like spirits from another dimension. It could just be the wind, making shadows. Moving curtains. I'm sure that's all it is. I pretend not to notice, but she smiles, and she knows that I do.

I am not the type of person who gives in to this sort of thing, spirit guides and goblins lurking about. I have never professed to visualize anything paranormal, but in their company, there is a certain something, a presence, of angels and guides, expanding the universe. I feel lifted, floating, circling in a parallel universe, not familiar, but not so unfamiliar either.

The living room lends itself to all things spiritual. Where furniture should be, there are musical instruments of every kind, guitars and bongos, huge glass bowls and soft hammers to pound out vibrations. When hit, the bowls actually vibrate in hums of various pitches, bouncing from wall to wall. A vibrational calling to gather lost souls and ancient warriors. Where most people would have a couch, a baby grand piano regally stands. In this house, the lack of furniture, and the accumulation of musical instruments seems as it should be.

Photography, original and beautifully edited, grace the open spaces, as do canvases of original oils, abstract except for one, left blank, waiting for inspiration. Rod's art has the aroma of still wet oil paint, while the house itself smells of beeswax candles and creativity, steeping tea and fulfilled dreams, vanilla fragrance and possibilities.

I feel both disconnected and connected at the same time, half in and half out of reality, with one foot securely planted in my world, and one foot venturing into theirs.

CHAPTER FOURTEEN

I am still well aware that there is the possibility that I am under some type of spell, that Rod and Jill are co-conspirators in a plot to twist my mind and control my thoughts. I already have no control over my thoughts. I talk about things I know nothing about, and cannot defend my position on carbonated beverages or junk food with any conviction, though I have been in love with both of these things all my life.

Just because I am entranced by my neighbors and their Houdini-magical house, doesn't mean I have given up all sense of logic and reason. I still do not understand how these people function. How friends just appear at their doorstep unannounced and are welcomed in, night after night. How food seems to multiply to accommodate the masses. How so much kindness permeates their space. They never seem to tire of constant interruptions and unexpected company. My entire concept of privacy seems outdated, and selfish.

I also do not understand their car situation. There are so many of them coming and going that I actually have no idea which car belongs to whom. At times, there is a silver-colored SUV in the driveway. Then a black Coronado, and a white Mercedes. The only predictable car is the Lexus station wagon, with a license plate containing the same numerals as my childhood home, and for that reason alone, I look away.

As it turns out, the white station wagon is the family car. The SUV is a rental that they often get when they have stuff they need to cart back and forth, or people that they need to taxi from one place to another. The black Coronado belongs to Linda, a frequent guest, long-time friend and documentary film maker. The white Mercedes belongs to Tracy, another long-time friend and founder of the local Montessori school. Two years later, when the black Harley Davidson trailer with the skull and crossbones shows up in the driveway I barely give it notice.

None of it matters. None of it is of any consequence. What matters is that I find myself shifting, elevating, stretching mentally to reach a higher plane of consciousness. I am enamored by the fact that Rod buys organic vegetables and offers me soy milk. That he grows his own herbs and places them at our doorstep. I am intrigued that they are plugged in to the absolute latest facts on the internet, on topics ranging from world strife to delta waves. They can speak intelligently about Heath Cliff, and the ancient pyramids. They do not discount UFO sightings, or corruption in the legal system. They have knowledge as well as opinions on any given area, and fact-check anything and everything on the internet to bolster their claims. Technology is their primary language.

They have a unique way of entertaining. It is as if they are their own guests, rather than host and hostess. They aren't rattled by turmoil, or a menu-change at the last minute. They entertain effortlessly, without bother, with wine and freshly cut flowers. They feel no need to entertain their guests. No planned events or seating arrangements. Every night is come as you are, bring nothing but yourselves, plan on having a good time. There are no rules, no stress, no sense of obligation that comes with having company. They simply believe that everyone is free to move about as they wish, and it is not up to them to force controls of etiquette among their guests.

They preach, as well as practice, independent thought. That as human beings we are free to behave and think any way we care to, within reason, and although most of us do not exercise that right, we should. I am beginning to think more broadly, laterally and vertically.

But what isn't happening is the book. Not because I am not writing day and night. I am just not writing right.

CHAPTER FIFTEEN

When I tell you the book isn't coming along fast enough, I am not being clear. In actuality, it isn't coming along at all. Two months have now become six, and I am beginning to doubt everything. I question my writing ability. I question Jill's commitment to the project. I question how I got myself mixed up with these people.

So, I continue to write bad stuff. Jill continues to speak in code. She really is starting to get on my nerves. I am starting to get on my nerves.

Jill never criticizes my work. Really. Never. Even when I turn in absolute garbage on paper, she extracts something good. A sentence, a phrase. Even one word. This, to me, is extremely unnerving. I try to find her breaking point. I test her patience. I urge her to give me the bottom line. To quit talking in circles. I am exhausted from trying to interpret her sentences. Just say it, I think. Say whatever is on your mind and be done with it. Then we can pick up the pieces and go on.

The frustration I feel is aimed inward. My lack of patience, my inability to understand the task at hand, my ineptness at rallying the troops. When I tire of that, I target the culprit as the book itself. The sheer concept of ridding oneself of negatives in a stress-filled world, doing good deeds and paying it forward. Shouldn't we all be doing that already? Are we such a selfish bunch that we have to read a book to find out how to be selfless?

Finally I conclude that the problem is Jill. Not Jill my friend who I care about, but Jill who continues to be dissatisfied, who forces me to push beyond my capabilities. I am mad at her. The chapters I write, the words I arrange just so on the page. What does she think? I mean, words just don't arrange themselves.

I am putting forth as much effort as can possibly be asked of me, and in the process, I am becoming increasingly angry. Although my efforts are not rejected, they are not hitting the mark either, and any writer, I believe, will agree that there is no separation between the writer and the writing. It is personal.

Now, I have to question my abilities, which is about as personal as one can get. My thoughts begin to spiral downward rather quickly. I wonder why I ever thought I should put myself in this situation, why I ever thought I was equipped to tackle this task, why I ever thought I had something of value to say. For those of you who fancy yourselves as writers, you understand exactly where I am coming from. If not, trust me on this, writing is enormously difficult work with the outcome almost never good enough. So as of today, I have decided to stop writing. This book for sure, if not all future writing. I will find something else to do with my life. Something that is less grueling, less emotionally taxing. Tomorrow I plan to tell Jill that I am no longer interested in writing her book. Tomorrow I quit.

But then I get a reprieve. A 12th hour pardon by the writing gods. A late night phone call from Jill, who has read what feels like my hundredth rewrite of chapter one and actually likes it! I am soaring, flying high. I am a writer after all. I can do good work! People should read what I write! My words can change the world! I think of quitting my day job immediately and dedicating the rest of my life to writing. I imagine the disappointment of my co-workers, but this is something that can benefit all of mankind. I will change the course of the entire human race.

I bask in this glory for a few days, but it is short-lived. Unfortunately, chapter two faces the same initial fate as chapter one. Jill only gives it a mediocre thumbs-up. She doesn't really feel that it says what it needs to say. She doesn't believe it captures the essence of Satori. Well guess what, Jill? I say under my breath. Neither do I. I don't capture the essence of Satori. I don't feel peaceful or harmonious. My head is swirling with negativity, namely why I ever volunteered to take on this project. You, I think, are perfectly capable of writing this book entirely on your own. Only you know what you are talking about. You haven't let me in on the secret. I want out. I don't say this out loud, of course. If she actually possesses super-powers, let her read my mind.

This project, I think, is going to self-destruct. But there is one thing. I actually like the idea of Satori. I believe in Satori. I have always lived Satori, long before I met Jill. And I like what I write. In defiance, I disregard her sentiments and move on to Chapter Three. Secretly. At night, while she sleeps, I write. I feel vindicated by my sneakiness.

The manuscript has some volume to it now. I carry it around with pride, despite her. She sweetly agrees that it is moving along nicely, but her tone of voice speaks differently. Too bad, I think. You aren't going to have the last word. Just because of this, I am not going to buy organic vegetables at the farmer's market, and I am not going to drink soy milk either. Instead I pop open a can of soda, and spend the afternoon polishing off a large bag of potato chips, followed by three bars of chocolate. These are some screwed up people.

CHAPTER SIXTEEN

Let me begin by retracting everything I said in chapter fifteen. There is no sinister plot to derail my writing ability. Jill has not put a curse on me. In fact, I am surprising myself with my accomplishments. I get it. Inadvertently her inability to move on makes me a much more proficient writer. Each time she turns down a chapter, I plunge to a deeper, more meaningful level. Even Rod is being as supportive as he can. I am going to have to develop thicker skin or less ego. Probably both.

Rod has begun his nightly ritual of cooking fresh fish, vegetables and homemade berry pies topped with whipped cream and delivering it to our door. According to Jill, he does this so I can commit myself to writing. I think he does it because he's a really nice guy. Also, because Jill has no doubt told him she is pushing me toward a nervous breakdown. We haven't actually spoken about it, but every time she sees me, she uses the tone of voice one uses when talking someone down from a ledge.

Rod also made a peace sign, identical to theirs, and delivered it to my front door. A peace offering from them to me. A mea culpa for pushing me over the edge. I accept it gratefully. He hangs it on the house, a twin to its brother right next door. He replaces our rusty gate hinges. He hammers the loose boards on the dock. He rebuilds our gate. Hawk pulls in our garbage cans after the trash men come. Jill revamps my computer so that it is updated. I don't know what is going on. But I do know I am not proud of my earlier temper tantrums. I also know I have to gather myself into my human form, and act much nicer.

In our down time, the space between writing and rewriting, Rod sticks to his organic health food diet, but Jill shares my love of soda and chocolate. She sneaks over several times each week and gulps down one, sometimes two, large glasses. I promise not to tell, but I think Rod is on to us. Still I will never divulge her secret. This makes us closer. Junk food has become our bonding agent.

Once, when she was sick, I brought her food. Chicken soup. It helped. A few days later, I brought a liter bottle of soda and a bowl of chocolates. We smuggled them into her bedroom and under the covers. I don't know how many chocolate bars she ate, but the next day there was color in her cheeks, a nice rosy glow, the glow that can only come from doing something covert.

Jill and I are good. We have come to an understanding. We are a well-oiled machine, synchronized, working together for the common goal. For the most part. Occasionally she irritates me by missing a deadline, and I rebel by swearing off the project, again. My thoughts are so volatile I begin to wonder if I have some sort of mental affliction. This is what bad writing does. I stay shut down, closed in, hiding in my own house. I purposefully avoid her for a day. A day feels too long. I miss her. Soon, I can't even remember why I was frustrated. I call her and we begin again.

Still, the book hasn't progressed in an acceptable fashion. At least not to me. She sees the flaws. Now, so do I. She is right. She, of course, has been right all along. She expects more of me. She tries to encourage me. You can do better, she says. I can't, I say. I have nothing more. You do, she says. I know you do. Her words haunt me, and I am once again stumped. How will I find my muse? What will stop my self-loathing? My consumption of junk food increases alarmingly.

Then one day, Jill leaves on a trip. This is not an unusual circumstance. She has gone on many short trips since I have known her. A few days here, and a few days there. This time she has work in Denmark. A movie. She is going to be gone for several weeks. Good, I think. Maybe I can have the book completed before she gets back. Maybe I can surprise her with a finished copy. I look forward to her absence.

But surprisingly everything comes to a screeching halt. I can't work without her. I have no direction. My mind is empty. After several weeks, I have nothing to show of the book. The problem isn't her, at all. The problem is me.

This is the first realization of life without her. Thoughts swirl in my head. What if I had never met her? What if she never comes back? I walk to the street each morning for the newspaper. I am in my pajamas, but no one is there to greet me. I don't want to be without her. I need her to come back.

When she finally returns, I am jubilant. I love my life, my job, my car, my clothes. I am on a manic high. I believe that everything is right with the world, and I have returned to normal. Dinners once again arrive at my front door, Bird Boy drags in garbage cans in the afternoon, and tea is blended and steeped. But something has changed. Something so small that I can't make it out. A subtle knocking in my brain, barely a concern worth noticing, conceived in the weeks without Jill. It is a warning. A news alert. Pay attention, it says. "No!" I say. Prepare yourself, it says. I hold my ears. But I can't block out the reality of what is to come. Instinctively I feel it. It is the beginning of the end.

CHAPTER SEVENTEEN

In the next few months I make further assessments about the people next door. They actually do work. As in, they have real jobs, employment. But they don't go to the office like the rest of the world. They don't have to punch a time clock, or account for their whereabouts. They simply work from home. They have deadlines like the rest of us, but they can work in their pajamas while they eat breakfast, or at night, with a nice glass of wine. They are able to bring their laptops to the beach and meet their obligations while they tan. It seems unfair to me that my life is embossed in a day planner, and theirs is created as they wish.

I want to be them. Spend the day going to the beach, and then stay up all night with the stars. I want to make conference calls in my pajamas in the middle of my living room. I want to sit around and think up creative ideas all day long, and then sell them. No wonder they're so happy. They are immersed in what they love to do and how they want to live.

I can't live like that, can I? Not in the life I have carved out for myself. Not in my world where the majority of people have to answer to a higher power, an employer, a supervisor, a timecard. Then again, I have a weekly paycheck to count on. I don't have to sell myself and hope that my worth is valued. No, that sort of life won't work for me. I'd be a nervous wreck living in their world. Then again, I am a nervous wreck living in mine.

CHAPTER EIGHTEEN

Rod has his opinions about the first three chapters of Satori, which do not coincide with Jill's. There seems to be invisible boundary lines that I haven't seen before, and when he crosses them, at least when she perceives he does, she does not mince words. She finds them. She uses them. He does not have to decode her sentences. So what is the problem with her communication with me? Why can't she criticize me?

Then it comes to me. Quite simply, I am her friend. In her mind, I can do no wrong. He is her husband. No latitude for husbands. Over years they have eked out an understanding of roles. Between Jill and me, the lines blur. Nothing is black and white. Images gray. Our friendship is cementing daily. Every stumble gets a hand up, any weariness by one is carried by the other.

Just about this time she says something that gets my attention. Something I can finally relate to. Something that changes the course of the book, and ultimately, the course of my life. She says that she notices I am writing from a place inside my head, where logic resides. Satori doesn't live there, she says. Satori lives in your heart. Write from your heart, she says.

Something that simple, permission to allow myself to open my heart and free the words that live there, changes everything. Immediately I feel different, better. I smile more, I seek people out, I offer a helping hand, I am genuinely concerned for their happiness. Satori is not only words on a page. Suddenly, the words come alive, in my life, every single day. Jumping off the bleachers and showing up on the field is powerful. You can do no wrong, if your heart is open.

So, that is why Jill and Rod are so content. Why their son beams happiness. Why people seek them out, want to drop by, spend time in their presence. Mystery solved. There is no witchcraft going on. No wizardry taking over. They are connected to each other from heart to heart to heart.

CHAPTER NINETEEN

If I haven't made this clear, let me do so now. I firmly believe that Rod, Jill and Hawk are gypsy-reincarnates from another life. They think nothing of packing up the car, getting in, and driving thousands of miles several times a year, to see friends, to work, to just go. In the same way you and I might go to the corner store for a loaf of bread, they jump on the highway and drive.

Sometimes Jill mentions their departures ahead of time, other times I pick up the signs. With Jill, I am a detective, always looking for clues. A rented SUV, bags waiting to be loaded in the driveway, friends coming over for a farewell dinner party, the dog temporarily adopted out. The grass cut shorter than normal, the sounds of excitement filling the air.

Their air, that is. My air is filled with something else. My air is filled with despair. Truly, I feel anxiety. I worry that they won't return. Every time they leave, I am consumed with a sinking feeling. A premonition. Mental anguish of losing the family I have grown to love. I trap her at her car. Promise that you'll come back, I say. I will, she says. But do you really promise? I ask in desperation. Yes, she says, but not convincingly.

I can't explain what her absence feels like. The circle has no life. It is dark, and dreary. A shadow of itself. I force myself to walk past her house while she is away, practicing for the possibilities that it might one day happen, that she might one day leave me forever. I feel the empty space, and stare at the empty house. It has no soul without her. I stare at the shuttered windows, the empty driveway. I feel sad. I want to feel bad. I want to wallow in my own misery for the day she really goes and doesn't come back. There is that sound again. The knocking in my head, louder this time. I put my hands over my ears in an attempt to shut out the message, but it's there just the same.

While she is gone, I take advantage of her absence as an opportunity to buckle down. Now that I know the secret of an open heart, chapter four seems right, chapter five flies out of me, six and seven soar in tandem. My heart bursts with excitement, finally freed from the constriction of over-thinking. My emotions race forward, eager to take first place. They implore people to change, ask them to find happiness, challenge them to take risks, and beg them to open their hearts.

It is said that the teacher cannot teach until the student is ready to learn. I am ready. Each chapter maps out my own personal growth, my own awakening, and my eagerness to share what I have learned. These people, the handyman, Julie, and Bird Boy represented who I was, but my friends, Rod, Jill and Hawk, represent who I have become. I have judged them unfairly. I have allowed my own biases and preconceived notions to stand in the way of the truth, blinding me from them, and the happiness they were destined to bring to me.

Satori is without judgment. It delights in self-growth. It is a master of positive self-esteem. Satori is the mirror to my soul. This book is simply a way for the universe to deliver that message. That is why Jill moved next door. That is why she said she needed her book written. That is why a writer and a movie producer became unlikely friends in such a short time. It was not serendipity. It was not by chance, but by design, that Jill waited until the exact right moment to come into my life. There are forces at work, all right, but it is not witchcraft. It is a life lesson that comes in some form to all of us, if we are open to receive it.

CHAPTER TWENTY

When the second summer approaches, and our book, Satori, is well under way, Jill mentions she cannot bear another season cramped into the little house with its faulty air conditioning and insufficient light. She says it offhandedly, inconspicuously. Quietly, in a way most people would not notice, but I do. So this is the anxiety. This is the knocking.

Let's go look at the house down the street, I say. It's unoccupied, for sale. And only two blocks away. If no one is going to live there, why can't Jill take up residence? Why can't she move in?

That is the goal. I can think of nothing else. We find the owner's name and call him, without response. We email him with no reply. He lives out of state, I say. Just move in. He won't know the difference. If he comes back, then you'll simply move out again.

As friends do when illogical ideas mushroom into wonderfully exciting scenarios, Jill and I imagine the possibilities daily. No matter that Rod tries to be the voice of reason. No matter that breaking and entering is a crime. To me, it is a perfect idea. They can move close by, still within walking distance.

This is our new mantra. Move into the empty house. Move in now. Even Rod loosens up under our prodding, and comes with us one day. We walk stealthily around the abandoned house, peeking in windows, imagining the possibilities. We discover another plus. It is completely furnished. If and when they are discovered squatting in the neighbor's house, they can simply carry their personal belongings back to the little house, and, no damage done. Well, other than trespassing, breaking and entering, and possibly identity theft, which, in my opinion is a stretch, because no one wants to actually *become* the owner, but it will be necessary to use his name in order to turn on the electric, cable and water.

To Rod, the idea of living in someone else's house without permission is, without question, ridiculous. To Jill, it is a wish, where anything is possible when that wish is cast into the universe. For me, it is the only plan I can think of to ensure that Jill won't move away. This is my sole reason not to lose sight of the goal. Months pass by without a word from the owner. The grass grows tall, the lawn maintenance crew, who tell me they have not been paid in months, finally quit. The cable company disconnects the wires. Mail no longer arrives. All signs points to the owner's abandonment of the property. Or untimely demise. That might not be too bad.

Under normal circumstances I would feel deep compassion for a man that is either sick or dead, but this is a case of survival. This is an extreme exception for which I expect to be forgiven. I am burdened by great disdain for him. I say unkind words under my breath each time I pass his house, about his selfishness, his greed, his utter rudeness.

I am a one woman complaint department. Out of spite, and because he refuses to play the game according to my rules, I report him to the town hall. I cite his lack of maintenance of his property, his failure to keep his lawn under control, his overall blight on the neighborhood. I feel good about this, even though it causes me several sleepless nights.

Surely this will secure the house for Jill. Days pass. One morning I hear the sound of a lawn mower. I walk down the street and see the maintenance crew. They're back, working on the house with vigor. By noon the yard looks pristine. I am completely devastated.

CHAPTER TWENTY ONE

You don't have to tell me I sound crazy. I already know that. I'm not entirely out of my mind, but that doesn't mean much right now. The fear of losing this friendship that has me unplugged. I am not myself. Without question, I have never considered the idea of taking possession of someone else's house, or identity, or any number of other things that have recently crossed my mind, but these are chaotic times, and I can't think straight. Spring is already here in full bloom. The dreaded summer is right around the corner.

Meanwhile, our book is finally completed! Two months have become nearly two years, but the result is worth it! We look at the finished product, hold it in our hands, admire Rod's handiwork with the book cover, and marvel over the contents. It is fair to say that whether anyone else reads it or not, we are in love with it, and that is all anyone could ask.

We convince ourselves there is nothing else like it. The original cover, the meditation music stuffed inside a pouch on the last page, the lessons at the end of each chapter. We are giddy with accomplishment. And destined to be rich. Filthy, stinking rich! As far as I am concerned, the anonymous owner can keep the house. With the money we make, Jill can buy the entire block, with money to spare. We dream of who we could give it to, who we could help. Our children of course, but then there are unmarried, pregnant women and old people with no teeth. People who are hungry and homeless. Children in need of clothes and toys, and families in need of a vacation. Animals in need of food and shelter. Yes, all that money will do a lot of people a lot of good.

I don't mind telling you there are a few people who won't be on my benevolence list, so called friends who have spoken about me disparagingly behind my back, or those who abandoned me during our hurricane cleanup. I fantasize about the way they will feel when they get short-changed, when no money comes their way. I find myself unusually happy about cutting them off, but I don't express this to Jill, because it isn't very Satori-like. Instead, I stick to the business at hand.

How will we market our book? I ask. I'm not sure, she says. Will people be able to find it? I ask. No, probably not, she says. Then, how will people buy it? I ask. They won't, she says. And just like that, my drunken dreams disappear into the ethers.

 *Chapter Twenty Two*

Jill is a good friend. She might not be perfect for everyone, but she is perfect for me, and that is about as good as anyone can ask for when they go through life. I feel as though we have been together forever, and maybe we have. Maybe we have been recycled over and over, until we don't even have to speak and yet we still know each other's thoughts. All I know is she makes me happy. Knowing she is right next door makes me happy. I don't have to see her, or even talk to her, but I like to know that in case I *need* to see her or talk to her, she's there. That's enough for me.

I attend her dinner parties often. In fact, I consider myself a regular. I am accepted by her friends, the ones who know how to locate anything on the computer, and who introduce me to YouTube. The ones who, even though they barely know me, come to my house with a birthday cake. These are the kind of people Jill and Rod attract. These are the kind of people I want in my life.

They bring me crystals for healing and cleansing, and forty varieties of teas. There is a wrapped deck of Tarot cards and a book to interpret them, in the event I want to expand my mind on that level. If not, there is a huge bar of chocolate to expand my waistline. And a pendant to use on my spiritual journey. Hawk constructs a statue made of paper clips, and Rod doesn't scrunch up his face in disdain when I pour a second glass of soda. Gifts for the soul, straight from the heart.

It is both curious and refreshing to notice that they don't speak about each other negatively. There are no sarcastic barbs slung behind their backs, no sideward glances to the others, when one of them makes a foolish statement. It is the type of idealized friendship that is found in storybooks and fantasies, and yet, it is being enacted in real time. The walls of their circle are always expanding as they welcome more people in, with the only requirements non-judgmental support and love. I am humbled by their acceptance.

CHAPTER TWENTY THREE

By now you can see my dilemma. I will never find people like these again, ever. Crazy weird, and crazy normal. Crazy mine. I love them. The days are growing warmer, announcing summer. I am on the verge of panic. They are going to take a trip, Jill says. Just for a few weeks. Her face looks wrong. It is the face of someone avoiding the truth. It is a lying face. The knocking in my head is deafening, begging me to do something.

I need Jill. She pulls me back from the black hole of commitment and responsibility. She picks me up when I've made a blunder, brushes me off, and makes everything better. She sees me as the person I am, not the titles I wear.

Mother, Grandmother, Wife. These labels are part of me, but not the whole of me. She sees the whole of me.

I make her promise to come back. I will, she says. When? I say. Maybe by July, she says. Maybe after the fourth. Her face is wrong again. She tells another lie. But not the kind of lie that is said with maliciousness. The kind of lie that serves to spare me. The kind of lie I have to forgive.

This is only May. I can't imagine two months without her. Two whole months. I blame the selfish owner of the other house. He should have let her move in, or house-sit. He could have made arrangements, I feel paralyzed, unable to come up with a solution, unable to solve this problem. I am angry at everyone for no apparent reason, dissatisfied with my job, disenchanted with my path, where all roads circle back to Florida. The state that hangs off the map like an afterthought. Too hot summers, unbearable humidity, monstrous size palmetto bugs, killer lightening, hurricane threats, and snowbirds crowding the roadways during the winter months, our only salvageable climate. And now this. Florida without Jill.

I barely remember life without Jill. I am of two minds. One mind reasons that it will only be two months until her return, but the other mind knows better. The other mind has already begun to grieve.

 **Chapter Twenty Four**

I reflect back to our times together. We had so much fun. Dinner parties and talks of substance. Silliness and belly laughs. Fishing late at night and swapping scripts. One whole evening playing dress-ups for an upcoming party of hoity-toity people unable to appreciate the depth of Zen tee shirts and peace bracelets. Draping her in my shoes and boots and evening gowns. She is willing to risk their criticism. I cannot let that happen to her.

We trash the house with sparkly sweaters and evening bags, blouses with plunging necklines and too tight pants. Silk skirts that cascade to the floor. To hell with them, those superficial imposters. She will wear diamonds and pearls. And animal fur. No animal fur, she begs. But you must, I say. Look at how gorgeous you are in this coat. I am, she says, aren't I? But she take it off on principle. She's right, of course. No animal fur.

Rod is summoned to carry the stash home. His face screams his disappointment. Materialism! He says. Yes, it is. But she must be prepared for battle. The wealthy can be so ruthless.

Jill knows people. Famous people. People who fly into town on private jets and buy buildings on a whim. People who introduce her to other famous people, with pictures to prove it. It doesn't impress her. She's had a lifetime of that, before Rod. He's had a lifetime of that, before her. Those days were burdens, they say. They stand in the way of true happiness. They choke you, and rob you of precious time and free thinking. They agree, those days once owned us.

I believe that. I have never needed wealth. But money, now that's different. I would not want to give that up. I hope I never have to. I am simply not that brave.

She beats to the sound of her own drum. She does not care about   controlling either situations or people. She cannot be controlled. She believes that each individual is free make their own choices, to eat or to fast, to wake or sleep, to move ahead or stay planted.

Once, in the midst of one of her dinner parties, while Rod whipped up delicious entrees and homemade desserts, and the guests mingled inside and out, Jill sat on the porch glider, knitting a scarf twice her height, and a matching purse. I didn't even know she could knit. There is still so much to learn.

One night Rod offers to teach me how to play the guitar. I had a guitar in nursing school. Then another one right after my fourth child was born. I had one when the kids went off to school, and again when they graduated college. Different guitars at different stages of my life, all waiting to be played. My bucket list consists of many things, but spoon bending and guitar-playing are near the top. I have recently bought another guitar, I tell Rod. Go get it, he says.

He is a good teacher. I have no idea how to hold it. How to find the strings. How to separate them with my fingers. How to position it without contorting my entire body. I am already frustrated. It's too big for me, I say. I don't think so, he says. I need to learn on a child's guitar, I say. He smiles. I complain that my back hurts. I complain about the ridges in my finger tips. He hands me a pick and I throw it down. I don't want a pick, I say. I just want to play the guitar. I say that I am tired, achy, miserable. He looks at me the same way he looks at Hawk when he misbehaves. I can't stand the sound of myself.

Will you practice? he asks. Yes, I say. Every day. Without strumming, there is no music, he says. I know, I say. I can do it. We begin with one chord. E. It is the only chord I know. It is the last chord he will ever teach me. I can still force my fingers to find the proper strings, but what's the point?

Technology doesn't like me. Its concepts escape me, they don't compute. Jill believes I am resisting. Maybe so. An unconscious rebellion toward the twenty-first century. The

100

twentieth was better. Simpler. People were nicer. People kept their word. Manufacturers tried their best. Automobiles were built strong. Medication didn't come with side effects of cancer, or death. Children were respectful. The world felt safer. Jill says I have to get over it. I have to catch up, or be left so far behind I will be lost forever.

She convinces me to subscribe to the internet. She says I am the only person on the planet who doesn't have it. It opens a whole new world to me, though I am partial to the old world. The smell of books on shelves, the feel of them in my hands. The thrill of researching a definition in the dictionary or fact finding through the encyclopedia. I love the smell of libraries. I love that they are orderly, books alphabetized on every shelf. I feel sorry for children who will never have the same need to visit one. I don't even know if they still teach the Dewey Decimal System. I love the Dewey Decimal System.

Jill is a natural born teacher. She teaches about patience and tolerance, timing and kindness. She's good with emotions and good with what I have always considered the necessities of life. Things you don't want to learn, but do anyway. Jill taught me how to cut and paste. Before that, when something was out of order, I spent hours retyping the entire document. Cutting and pasting should not be minimized. It is one of the great wonders of the technological world.

I love to cut and paste. It gives me a feeling of power. It keeps my computer guessing, off center. With the click of the mouse, it must obey me. I am in control. Sometimes I write things out of order and then force my computer to make it right, just for fun. I wish there was a computer to make the world right. A computer that enforces universal peace. Now that would be something.

I love the freedom of walking over to Jill's house and opening the door without knocking. It is so decadently rude, so invasively improper, and yet, it feels so right. There are no pauses in conversations when I walk in. No sideward glances conveying annoyance. Nothing to indicate an inconvenient interruption. They keep no secrets from me. Except one.

 ## Chapter Twenty Five

I am becoming a nuisance, showing up all times of the day and night, incessantly calling, walking over, for no apparent reason. Then I keep my distance. I don't call Jill at all. I don't acknowledge her e-mails. I try to find a way to be angry at her, to erase her from my memory, to dump her in the midst of all my other disappointments and be done with it. But at night, when she isn't looking, I walk past her house. I take it all in. I stand there listening to my racing heart. I can't swallow. I can't take a deep breath. The whole of me is burdened. My feet can barely shuffle home.

The light in their windows signifies activity. It is late. They should be sleeping. The blinds are drawn but I can see through them with my mind. I see them packing. I feel them leaving. I can't think of a way to stop them.

I bury myself in my next book. Jill is my cheerleader and biggest fan. Again, we meet every day in the circle. Again, she reads my work. This time she calls each day with enthusiasm. She is in love with Grace, my main character. She needs more, she says. Tell me more. She promises it will be a good book. Maybe even a movie. Can I produce it? she asks. I don't answer. Will you send me the rest of the chapters while I am away? she asks. Again, I don't answer. I can't. My sorrow has rendered me mute.

She thinks I am angry with her. I don't come over as much. I don't want to see her bags packed. I don't want to know her plans. All that I already know is enough. She will spend the summer in the Midwest, Hawk will have cousins to play with, Jill and Rod can secure property. I have never been to the Midwest. I don't even know where it is on the map. But I imagine her there. Making new friends, good friends. Friends who make her forget about me.

Rod cuts the grass extra short. He weeds, and putters around the yard. He tells me to help myself to the herbs and vegetables that are still growing out back, but I won't. It won't be the same.

It's the morning of the last day. I consider calling Jill to meet me in the circle. To give her the next chapter of Grace. But I don't. It's too painful. If she's leaving, then she should just go.

I sneak over to her car. The last of the manuscript is tucked underneath her windshield wiper. She'll find it. She'll know what it means. I am a coward. It is the only way I know to say good bye.

A flood of tears stream down my face, inconsolable, sobs that come from somewhere I can't locate. Running, my slippers kick pebbles in the driveway, a stone placed on the gravesite of our friendship. She doesn't see me. Good. I close the front door. I can't see her either. Not anymore.

I dress and race to my car, a quick getaway. She has placed something wedged up inside my car door handle. A refrigerator magnet. A poem about forever friends. It speaks to me. I half expect her to be standing nearby, but she is nowhere to be found. We are the same. She is a coward too.

 **CHAPTER TWENTY SIX**

Our street is nearly empty. Vacant houses. Jill's absence is more obvious at night. Mine is the only light on the street. I walk the circle in darkness. I am afraid of the dark. I am afraid of what I can't see. I am afraid of what I know. I am afraid to be without her. She never leaves her house unlit. Never. Until now. This time they don't plan on returning for a long time, if ever.

I peek in the window and see furniture. That's something. I hold on to that. No one moves away forever and leaves their things. But Jill might. Jill might shed her skin and not look back. No matter how I try to discount it, I know it's true. By the fourth week of her absence, I am completely overwhelmed with the emptiness of her.

I walk past her house and hear and see nothing. No laughter from the backyard. No cars strewn all over the driveway. No torches lighting the path to their door. I miss her so much. I miss Rod's music and the smells of gourmet food, the tow-head boy racing over with some new invention or piece of technology. I miss her wisdom, her smile, her presence. I miss her friends. I miss her stealing over for a quick gulp of soda and a pocketful of chocolates. I miss who I am when I am with her.

I walk past the other empty house, the one Jill could have lived in, the one that is just down a few blocks, and I am sad for both of us. Who knows what tragedies caused those people to move away. Who knows the sorrows of their lives. I know the sorrow of mine. I should not have thought such ugly things about those poor souls. Maybe they're homeless now. Maybe they died. I should have been nicer. I lost my way, out of desperation, and wished them ill. I am so ashamed.

One night becomes another, and still the same darkness. When I pass the empty house with the missing occupants, I talk out loud. Forgive me, I say. I'll pray for you. Then I come back to my block, to Jill's house. I whisper my secrets to her. I know she is not there, but it doesn't matter. I tell her anyway.

By the beginning of the second month I am desperate for some kind of contact. I email her. I tell her I miss her. I tell her about the neighborhood, and my new book. I tell her it is unbearable in this state without her. She doesn't respond. Not even once. I feel like I have really lost her.

I am nearly buried in the grieving process. I can't breathe under the unbearable weight of my own sadness.

 **CHAPTER TWENTY SEVEN**

Finally! I open my mailbox to find a letter from Jill! My car is parked in the circle, facing her house, facing the unlit peace sign. I half expect her to walk out her front door. I tear open the letter. She misses me. She will be home soon. She does not give me a date. I need a date. A point of reference. I need to mark off time, something to keep me centered. I need to see if she will keep her promise. A sense of urgency overtakes me. I have to find her. I have to know where she is right now. But the postmark is blurred! I can't make it out. My headlights illuminate the return address.

Jill Slane
Wherever the Wind Blows Me
USA

The return address sobers me into sudden clarity. There is nothing I can do to hold her back, to stop her from leaving. Jill cannot be captured by earthly manipulation or guilt. She cannot be coerced to change her course. Like all of us, she is a child of the universe. But she is more than that. She is also a promoter of peace, a keeper of secrets, a high priestess of a foreign celestial planet. She floats on clouds and sprinkles fairly dust. That she sprinkled some on me is enough.

 *Chapter Twenty Eight*

I am beginning to get the hang of this life lesson thing. People are not possessions. They are not meant to be held hostage by the insecure whims of someone else. They have work to do in this lifetime. They have somewhere they must be, something else they must learn, and someone else they must teach. Life is a series of forward motions.

Jill has work to do, and so do I. I have to let her go.

I feel more settled. I am no longer burdened by the same emotions as before. I still feel sadness, but not craziness, loneliness, but not desperation. Jill is a gift. Even gone, she influences my thinking, opens my heart, and in many ways changes my life. She has taught me Satori. She has offered something to take with me forever.

 *Chapter Twenty Nine*

Jill keeps her promise. She returns to Florida for one week at the end of August. Just enough time to pack her belongings for the final departure. Just enough time to say a proper good bye.

This time I am not a coward. I watch her gather her things to be later unpacked in a setting far away from anywhere I've ever been. I walk over every chance I have, to close any gaps and tie up loose ends. I take pictures of the moving van, photographs I will probably never look at again, but necessary to mark the close of this chapter. Frozen moments in time, Hawk carrying his Lego sets, Linda wrapping glassware, Chris, her husband, lifting one end of the dresser while Rod balances the other, and Jill, still smiling, still talking on the phone, still pursuing the next dream, just around the bend.

The truck is nearly loaded as dusk approaches. The peace sign is removed from the front wall of the house, the sign that marked the beginning of our journey. It is placed carefully inside the truck, wrapped in blankets. It is also placed carefully in my heart, wrapped in memories.

Take whatever you want, they say. Whatever we leave is yours. I do. I take Hawk's old surfboard, a broom from the garage, and some clay flower pots. I don't need them, but I want them.

We share a final cup of tea. One last discussion on the hazards of junk food, one last argument on the talents of Elvis. My eyes are filled with tears. Rod turns away, wiping his face. Jill hugs me tight and tells me she will hold the light for me. That she will look for deals, real estate deals. That maybe I can join them some day in Arkansas. I don't even know where Arkansas is, but I tell her to look for something, that someday I might come, that maybe we can once again be neighbors. I know it isn't true. I can't afford a house in

Arkansas. But I could win something, money or something. People win stuff.

I speak as if I am in emotional overdrive. Fragments fly, pieces of memory searching for other like memories, desperate to glue the story back together. It would be so easy to pretend this wasn't happening. That they were just leaving on another temporary vacation. But that would be a lie. And this friendship is the truth.

This is the story of my two years spent with Jill. It is also the coming to grips with middle age, facing losses, counting blessings, finding clarity, and most of all, personal growth. She may not be a witch, but she has magically changed my life in ways I could not have imagined. She has granted me permission to become me.

CHAPTER THIRTY

This is the first night that I have walked the circle since Jill has moved away. It's been more than two weeks. I look at the little house and feel the sadness of it. Soon, I think. Soon you will have another family loving you. Soon you will know the joy of occupants and visitors, fresh coats of paint and furniture. I know it is difficult to be laid bare, to be without window dressing. I feel the same way. We will learn together, I think. The little house and I. We will learn to wear our window dressing proudly, to show it off in public, to embrace it in private.

You should be called a cottage, I say. A cottage? it asks. I think it suits you, I say. The answer is soft, humble, and proud. Yes, I would like that.

No matter who else comes to live in the cottage, I will always think of it as Jill's house. I will always recall the laughter and the music, the friendships and the magic that the cottage witnessed. It is dark outside. Night. I walk up the path to the front of the house, to the place where the table used to be, the place where I would leave my manuscripts, held down by a stone, when she wasn't home.

Under the light of the moon, I see a reflection in the window. I imagine Jill's face, hear her sweet voice, and smell vanilla in the air. The reflection looks back. I can almost see her happy smile, but instead, I see mine.

EPILOGUE

If you ever come across Jill and Rod in your travels, and it is likely you will, take a moment to get to know them. Sit with them awhile, toast a glass of wine, and let them set a place for you at their table. Then you will know what I mean. Why it was so difficult to let go.

Before they left, Jill and Rod renewed their wedding vows. I was there. I think this, more than anything else I can tell you, says it all.

Jill Ann,

I want to renew my vows of complete dedication and love to you, my wife of 10 years. My partner of thousands of years.

I therefore add to the previous commitments to you that:

I will always be a loving, dedicated husband married to you from the inside out through the universal touch of all things, being God.

I will continue to see you spiritually first, and physically second.

I will give to both of us all of the knowledge and intellect that I have within me to keep our minds, our bodies and our essence well and healthy.

I will be with you in mind, body, spirit for all of existence and beyond.

I will continue to create more love through touch, through breath and through new unknown spiritual connections with you my Jill Ann.

I will continue to achieve the very best for you and for our family in my thoughts, my work, and my higher intuitions.

I will never hate. I will not cause anger, nor will I precipitate any negative action against you, in thought or in any other manifested form.

You may depend on my dedication and love to nurture both of us and feed our life with goodness, love, peace, and happiness for all time.

I dedicate these vows to you, my wife.

Marry me again for ever and always.

Roddy

Hold the light for me, Jill.

Laurie Elizabeth Murphy

ABOUT THE AUTHOR

Laurie Murphy is a Registered Nurse. For the past 26 years she has worked as a counselor, assisting her clients to face their challenges, seek resolution, and embrace change.

She and Jill Slane have co-authored *Satori, Keeping a Peaceful Heart in Chaotic Times*, Satori House Publishing, 2010.

She has also co-authored with Dr. Nadir Baksh, *In the Best Interest of the Child, A Manual for Divorcing Parents*, Hohm Press, 2006, *You Don't Know Anything, A Manual for Parenting Your Teenager*, Hohm Press 2007, and *8 Strategies for Successful Step-Parenting*, Hohm Press, 2009.

Cellophane Memories, her first book, Sparrow Heart Publishing, 1995, is currently out of print. It is expected to be available as an e-book in late 2012.

QUESTIONS FOR BOOK CLUB MEETINGS...

Why do you suppose the author was so cautious about embarking on a friendship?

Do you think the frustrations that surrounded their business relationship added to or subtracted from their friendship?

Do you believe that Jill purposely withheld chapter information so that the author could gain insight each step of the way?

Who do you consider to be the teacher in this book, the author or Jill?

Who do you believe suffered the greatest loss in the end?

What is your definition of friendship?

Have you taken the risk of opening your heart?

SPARROW HEART PUBLISHING
421 South East Martin Avenue
Stuart, Florida 34996

Made in United States
Orlando, FL
18 February 2024

43862462R00080